Oma's Quilt

For my mother, a wonderful oma — P.B.

To Clara, Antoine and Édith's
two wonderful grandmothers — S.J.

Text © 2001 Contextx Inc.
Illustrations © 2001 Stéphane Jorisch

Kids Can Press acknowledges the financial support of the Ontario Arts
Council, the Canada Council for the Arts and the Government of Canada,
through the BPIDP, for our publishing activity.

Published in Canada by
Kids Can Press Ltd.
29 Birch Avenue
Toronto, ON M4V 1E2

Published in the U.S. by
Kids Can Press Ltd.
2250 Military Road
Tonawanda, NY 14150

www.kidscanpress.com

The artwork in this book was rendered in mixed media.
The text is set in Celeste.

Edited by Tara Walker
Designed by Karen Powers
Printed and bound in Hong Kong, China, by Book Art Inc., Toronto

This book is smyth sewn casebound.

CM 01 0 9 8 7 6 5 4 3

Canadian Cataloguing in Publication Data

Bourgeois, Paulette
  Oma's quilt

ISBN 1-55074-777-0

I. Jorisch, Stéphane. II. Title.

PS8553.O85477O42 2001   jC813'.54   C00-932858-0
PZ7.B68Om 2001

Kids Can Press is a *Corus*™ Entertainment company

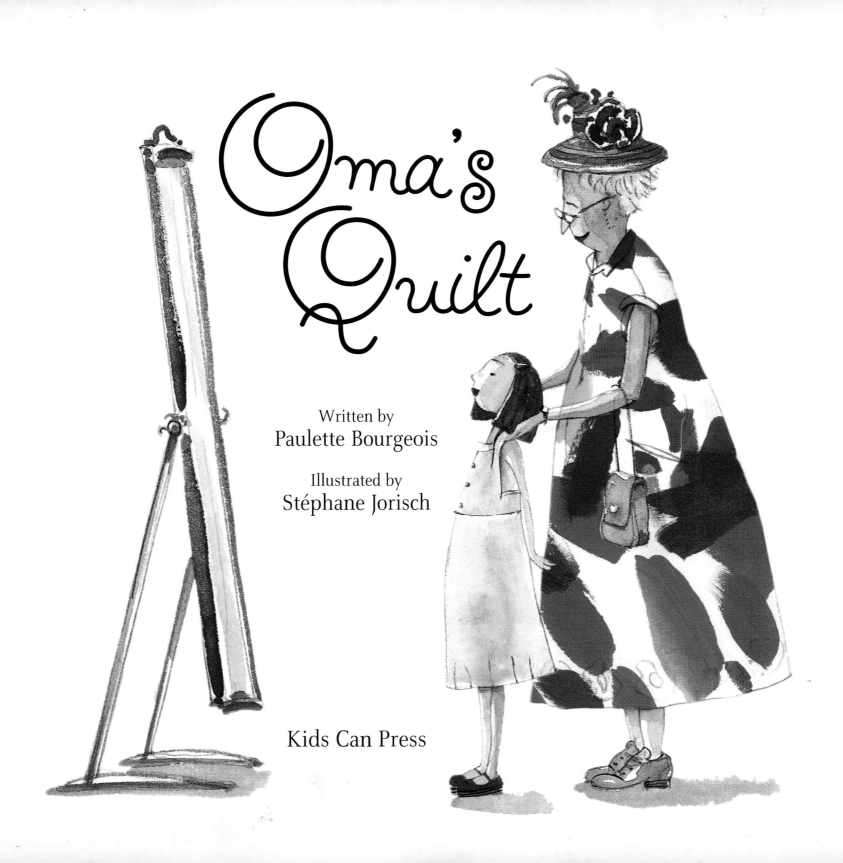

Oma's Quilt

Written by
Paulette Bourgeois

Illustrated by
Stéphane Jorisch

Kids Can Press

W e take one last look around my oma's house on Maple Street.

The house is empty, but it still smells like cabbage soup, warm yeasty dough, lemon polish and vinegar.

"I've lived here most of my life," says Oma.

"That's a long time," I say.

Oma's special things are packed away and stored in our basement. There are boxes and boxes because Oma never throws anything away. She keeps Opa's workshirts and her olden-day dresses. She saves ribbons and lace, curtains and bedspreads.

Oma stands in front of the kitchen window and looks out at the backyard.

"Emily. Oma. It's time to go," says my mother.

As we drive away, Oma keeps looking back.

Oma is moving into the Forest View Retirement Home.

In Oma's new room, my mother asks, "What do you think?"

Oma glances out the window at the river and the weeping willows.

"On Maple Street, there wasn't much to look at," she says. "But Mrs. Mostowyk always waved when she hung her laundry out to dry."

Together, we walk around the building. There's a big kitchen where a cook makes the meals.

My mother tells Oma that she doesn't have to cook anymore.

"I love to cook," says Oma. "Opa always said nobody makes strudel like I do."

"You can make strudel at our house," I say.

Oma smiles at me and pats the back of my hand.

I think Forest View is beautiful. There are flowers everywhere. There is
a room for painting and another for making pottery. There is a library and
a big bulletin board — and even bowling on Wednesdays!

Before we finish our tour, Oma says she is tired
and wants to lie down.

On the way home, my mother is very quiet.

"I don't think Oma likes it there," I say. "I think she misses Maple Street."

My mother looks like she is about to cry.

"Don't worry," she says. "Everything will work out."

And just like Oma, my mother pats the back of my hand.

Oma spends her days sitting in a chair in the corner of her room. She says the food tastes funny. Nobody knows how to make strudel and there are lima beans two times a week. She says she can't sleep at night in a strange bed. Oma calls the other old people a bunch of nincompoops.

"Nincompoops!" I laugh and roll the word around my mouth.

At home, my mother and I sort through Oma's things.

We are going to make two piles. Things to keep and things to give away.

"Can't we just keep it all?" I ask.

"Oh, Emily," says my mother, laughing.

"You are so much like your grandmother."

I try on old clothes and funny hats.

I show my mother a flannel shirt with paint on the cuffs. It belonged to my opa.

My mother strokes it softly.

"I can't imagine why Oma kept these kitchen curtains," says my mother.

I shrug. "Maybe they remind her of Maple Street."

"Look at this!" my mother says, holding up a raggedy blanket.

"It was yours when you were a baby, Emily."

We found the dress my mother wore for her first piano recital.

At the end of the day, we only had one pile. Things to keep.

There's one last box to sort. Inside is a faded quilt.

"Oma made this from Opa's worn-out shirts," my mother says.

"We could make a quilt," I suggest, "using all the things that Oma loved at Maple Street."

"Oh, Emily!" says my mother, giving me a hug. "What a clever, clever girl you are!"

We work on the quilt every day for weeks and
weeks. I learn how to cut evenly and sew straight.
The ends of my fingers are sore because
I prick them with the sharp needle.

"Look what you've got us into!"
says my mother.

But she is laughing for the
first time since Oma moved
away from Maple Street.

I want the quilt to be a surprise, but it's hard to keep the secret.

Oma keeps complaining. Her room is too cold in the day and too hot at night. The flowers in the hallway make her sneeze. The bowling alley lanes are crooked and the rental shoes smell funny.

"Don't worry, Oma," I say. "It will get better." Then I pat the back of her hand.

Finally, the quilt is finished.

I hold my breath as Oma takes the wrapping off the big box, lifts out the quilt and spreads it on her bed. She traces my stitches with the tips of her fingers.

My mother has embroidered a house like the one on Maple Street. There is an oven for baking bread and making strudel, and a window with curtains that looks out at Mrs. Mostowyk's house. Oma gives a little wave.

Oma tells me a story for each piece of fabric we've sewn in the quilt.
She remembers dancing at her wedding, counting time as my mother
played the piano and wrapping me in my blanket on the day I was born.
"The quilt is beautiful," Oma says. "It is made of love."

Oma still complains about the nincompoops. But she's heard that Mrs. Mostowyk might be moving into the building. On the cook's day off, Oma helps in the kitchen and makes cabbage soup and strudel. She even bought her own bowling shoes. Oma tells me that whenever she misses Maple Street, she wraps herself in her quilt and she feels right at home.